JEREMY'S DREIDEL

For Abba, who was a really good listener and
for Haya, who taught me about the fancy
equipment, and about so many other things.
– E.G.

To my baby, Pau, who keeps teaching me
about love every day.
– M.M.

KAR-BEN PUBLISHING, INC.
A division of Lerner Publishing Group, Inc.
241 First Avenue North
Minneapolis, MN 55401 U.S.A.
1-800-4-Karben

Website address: www.karben.com

Library of Congress Cataloging-in-Publication Data

Gellman, Ellie.
        Jeremy's dreidel / by Ellie Gellman ; illustrated by Maria Mola. — Rev. ed.
            p.   cm.
        Summary: A boy makes a Braille Hanukkah dreidel for his father, who is blind. Includes instructions for making
    different types of dreidels.
        ISBN: 978–0–7613–7507–4 (lib. bdg. : alk. paper)
        [1. Dreidel (Game)—Fiction. 2. Hanukkah—Fiction. 3. Handicraft—Fiction. 4. Blind—Fiction.
    5. People with disabilities—Fiction.] I. Mola, Maria, ill. II. Title.
    PZ7.G2835Je 2012
    [E]—dc23   2011029015

Manufactured in the United States of America
1 – PP – 7/15/12

JEREMY'S DREIDEL

BY **ELLIE GELLMAN**

ILLUSTRATED BY **MARIA MOLA**

KAR-BEN
PUBLISHING

Jeremy read the poster at the Jewish Community Center, then added his name to the sign-up sheet.

When he arrived at the art room on Monday, Jeremy recognized Abby, who used to be in his carpool. She was carrying a box of paper towel tubes and old magazines. David, a friend from swimming class, was looking through a book.

"Look at this," he called to Jeremy. "It's a black and white top that turns colors when you spin it. Do you think I can make a dreidel like that?"

"Sure you can," said a friendly voice.
"I'm Miriam, your workshop leader."

Everyone found seats around the table. "Before we start, what do you know about dreidels?" Miriam asked.

Adam spoke first. "It's a top we spin on Hanukkah."

"It has four Hebrew letters on it," Jeremy added. "*Nun, Gimel, Hey*, and *Shin*. They stand for *Nes Gadol Hayah Sham*, A Great Miracle Happened There."

"That's right." Miriam smiled. "Hanukkah celebrates the victory of the small Maccabee army over the huge army of Antiochus. That was a miracle."

"There was another miracle," said Jacob. "When the Maccabees lit the Temple menorah, a tiny jar of oil lasted for eight whole days. That's why we light candles for eight days."

"My name is Orit and I was born in Israel," said a girl with short, curly hair. "We call a dreidel a *sevivon*. The letters on my *sevivon* from Israel are different. They stand for A Great Miracle Happened *Here*."

"Now let's see what you all brought," Miriam said.

Abby emptied her bag. "I want to make my dreidel from recycled materials," she said.

Jacob had brought an old music box to make a singing dreidel. Matthew wanted to use a rubber ball, so his dreidel would bounce.

"What do you need for your dreidel?" Miriam asked Jeremy.

"Just clay," he said.

"Do you want to look through my science book for a more interesting idea?" David asked.

"No, thanks," Jeremy replied, as he returned from the supply closet with a lump of grey clay. "I have a great idea already. My dreidel is a surprise for someone."

Jeremy began rolling, pounding, and softening the clay.

David tried to keep his mind on sanding his wood, but he couldn't help looking over at Jeremy. He wondered what kind of surprise someone could make from a lump of clay.

Soon Adam became curious, too. He peeked over Jeremy's shoulder. "Look at this!" he called out. A group gathered around Jeremy, as he carefully molded tiny dots onto one side of his dreidel.

"What's that?" asked Jacob. "A secret code?"

Jeremy looked up. He was used to explaining.

"The dots are called Braille. It's a way of reading for blind people. This group of dots is a *nun*."

"I know about Braille," said Sally. "Blind people can't see the letters on a piece of paper, but they can feel dots with their fingers. The dots stand for letters, numbers, and words."

"Who do you know who is blind?" Adam asked Jeremy.

"It's for my dad," Jeremy answered.

"But your family doesn't have a guide dog," said Abby.

"Not all blind people have them," Jeremy answered patiently. "My dad uses a cane, so he doesn't bump into anything. And he has a tiny GPS that tells him when to turn right or left in a new place. "

"How can he help you with your homework?" wondered Orit.

"The same as any dad," explained Jeremy, "only with fancy equipment. He uses a laptop with tiny pegs that pop up and down to make the Braille letters. He can read exactly what I see on the screen, so he knows if I'm really working or if I'm playing a video game. If I send him a text message, his cell phone reads it to him."

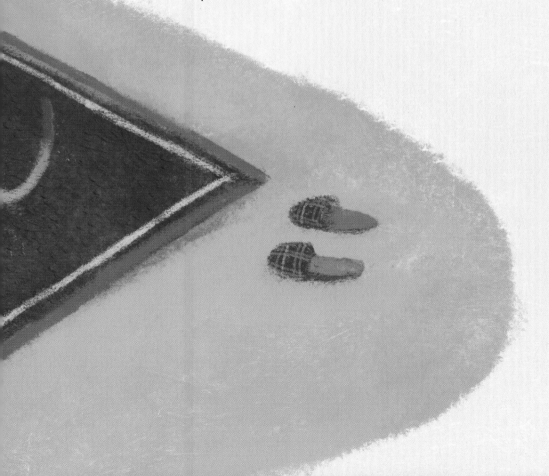

"But what does he do all day?" Matthew wondered.

"He goes to work, just like your mom and dad," said Jeremy. "And in his free time, he sings in the JCC choir. He loves to read. Sometime he reads in Braille and sometimes he listens to audiobooks."

"But when I come over to play, he always says, 'Hi,' and knows who I am right away," David insisted. "Besides, he doesn't look blind."

"Blind isn't how you look, it's how you see," Jeremy said. He was starting to get impatient. "And dad knows all my friends' voices. He's a really good listener."

Jeremy was relieved when Miriam said it was time to put the art supplies away. He didn't want to answer any more questions.

On Wednesday, Miriam made an announcement. "The art department wants to put some of your dreidels in the lobby showcase, but there is only room for three. Let's vote for the ones we like best."

A few minutes later, Miriam announced the winners: Jacob's musical dreidel, Abby's environmentally-friendly dreidel, and Jeremy's Braille dreidel.

Abby and Jacob beamed as the others congratulated them,
but Jeremy slid down in his seat.

"What's wrong, Jeremy?" asked Miriam, surprised at his reaction.

"You still don't understand," he said sadly. "My dad can't see my dreidel, and if it's locked behind glass, he won't be able to play with it, either."

The room was quiet. Then Abby said, "Jeremy is right. Why do we need our dreidels in a showcase? Dreidels are meant to be played with."

"Let's put up posters inviting people to join us in a dreidel game instead," Jacob suggested.

That Sunday, families gathered at the JCC for the Hanukkah celebration.
They enjoyed latkes and jelly donuts made by the cooking class. The drama
club put on a play about Judah Maccabee, and the choir sang Hanukkah songs.

The dreidel table was busy, as people picked up instruction sheets and joined in the games. Babies pulled the string on Jacob's dreidel to hear the music. Children sat in a circle to spin Abby's recycled dreidel.

And Jeremy sat with his father, smiling proudly as kids and grownups took turns playing with his Braille dreidel.

ABBY'S ENVIRONMENTALLY-FRIENDLY DREIDEL

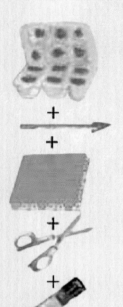

SMALL SIZE

You will need:

Empty egg carton

Dried out thin marker

*Pictures from newspapers,
 magazines or junk mail*

Scissors, glue, dark marker

Cut two cups from the egg carton and tape them together at the open sides to make a "ball." Glue decorative pictures over the cups, making sure to cover the places where the two cups meet. Let the decorations dry. With a dark marker, write the Hebrew letters Nun, Gimel, Hey, and Shin over the pictures, one on each side. Poke the thin marker thought the top and bottom of the ball. If the hole is too loose, reinforce it with tape. Let the point of the marker stick out a little on the bottom. Spin the dreidel and see which letter lands on top.

LARGE SIZE

You will need:

Empty milk carton, washed and dried

*Pictures from newspapers, magazines,
 or junk mail*

Dried out fat marker

Scissors, glue, strong tape, marker

Cut the milk carton about 3" from the spout. Bend the open spouts backwards, so that each side is flat against the carton. Tape them down. Open up the other side of the spout and bend those pieces backwards over the first. Tape them down as well. This should leave a point in the middle. Slide the spout half of the carton over the bottom half. Glue a collage of pictures on top of the cover. Let it dry and write the Hebrew letters on the sides of the dreidel. Make a hole in the flat end of the milk carton. Poke the marker through for a handle (it will not reach the other end).

MATTHEW'S DREIDEL BALL

You will need:
Old ball
   (small rubber, tennis, or foam ball)
Pen or pencil

Cardboard
Markers,
   scissors, glue

Cut a strip of cardboard about an inch wide, long enough to go around the ball with half an inch overlap. Mark off the half inch, and then fold the strip in half, and in half again to make four even sides. Draw a dreidel letter on each side of the cardboard. Wrap the strip around the ball and tape the flap down. Stick the pen into the top of the ball, letting most of it stick out on top. Spin the dreidel. It will roll and wobble and will eventually land with one of the letters on top.

DAVID'S SCIENCE PROJECT DREIDEL

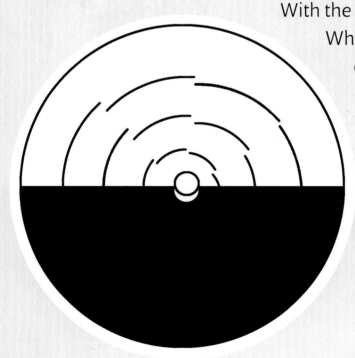

This dreidel uses an optical illusion called Benham's Wheel.

You will need:

Very short pencil with dull point

White cardboard circle or thin circle of wood sanded smooth

Black marker and light colored marker

4 small pieces of light colored paper

With the black marker, copy this pattern of Benham's Wheel onto your circle. Make a hole in the center of the circle, and poke the pencil through. Only a little point needs to stick out. With the light marker, write the Hebrew letters on the pieces of colored paper, and glue onto the circle. When you spin the top, the black and white pattern will show colored stripes. The letter you have spun is the letter on top.

HOW TO PLAY THE DREIDEL GAME

You will need a dreidel and enough nuts, candies, bottle caps, or pennies to give 10 to each player.

To start, each player puts one playing piece into the middle. The first player spins the dreidel. When it stops, look at the letter on top.

NUN means nothing. You take nothing and lose nothing.

GIMEL means get them all. You take everything in the pile.

HEY means half. You take half the pile. If there is an uneven number, you take half plus one.

SHIN (or **PEY** on an Israeli dreidel) means share or put. You must put another piece in the pile.

Any time all the pieces are gone, everyone must add one to the pile.

ABOUT BRAILLE

Braille letters are made by pushing out raised dots on heavy paper with a special Braille stylus. The number and position of dots changes for each letter. Each language has its own Braille alphabet. There are Braille books and magazines, and often Braille signs, elevator buttons, and captions in museum exhibits.

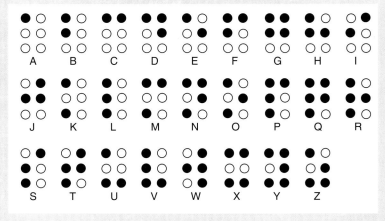

ENGLISH BRAILLE ALPHABET

Jeremy used the Hebrew Braille alphabet on his dreidel. Here are the letters he used:

NUN **GIMEL** **HEY** **SHIN**

ABOUT THE AUTHOR AND ILLUSTRATOR

ELLIE GELLMAN grew up in Minneapolis, where she first began telling stories to the children in her synagogue. She has taught in Jewish schools in the United States, Canada, and Israel. Her previous books include *Shai's Shabbat Walk, Tamar's Sukkah,* and *Justin's Hebrew Name.* She lives in Jerusalem and has four children and two grandchildren.

Born in Barcelona, Spain, **MARIA MOLA** was trained in the Francesca Bonnemaison School in Barcelona and the Moore College of Art in Philadelphia. She works in both traditional and digital media, often combining both. She lives with her husband and cat, Ghido, in Philadelphia.